W9-AMN-945

Scrapbooks of America™

Published by Tradition Books™ and distributed to the school and library market by The Child's World®
P.O. Box 326, Chanhassen, MN 55317-0326 ➥ 800/599-READ ➥ *http://www.childsworld.com*

Photo Credits: Cover: Stock Montage (map); Bettmann/Corbis: 12 (top), 13, 19, 27, 29, 35, 36–37, 38–39; Kevin Fleming: 7; Franz Xaver Habermann/Corbis: 24; Hulton-Deutsch Collection/Corbis: 33; Philadelphia Museum of Art/Corbis: 17; Corbis: 21; Kathy Petelinsek: 31; Stock Montage: 8, 9, 11, 12 (bottom), 14, 15, 28, 40

An Editorial Directions book
Editors: E. Russell Primm and Lucia Raatma
Additional Writing: Lucia Raatma and Alice Flanagan/Flanagan Publishing Services
Photo Selector: Lucia Raatma
Photo Researcher: Alice Flanagan/Flanagan Publishing Services
Proofreader: Chad Rubel
Design: Kathleen Petelinsek/The Design Lab

Library of Congress Cataloging-in-Publication Data
Dell, Pamela.
  Freedom's light : a story about Paul Revere's midnight ride / by Pamela J. Dell.
    p. cm. — (Scrapbooks of America series)
Summary: In 1775 in Boston, twelve-year-old Mary Cates, a silver polisher in Paul Revere's shop and a patriot, becomes a spy when she accidentally discovers that an apprentice is working against their boss.
  ISBN 1-59187-016-X (lib. bdg. : alk. paper)
  1. Revere, Paul, 1735-1818—Juvenile fiction. [1. Revere, Paul, 1735–1818—Fiction. 2. Spies—Fiction. 3. United States—History—Revolution, 1775–1783—Fiction.] I. Title.
  PZ7.D3845 Fr 2002
  [Fic]—dc21   2002004653

Scrapbooks of America™

FREEDOM'S LIGHT

A STORY ABOUT PAUL REVERE'S MIDNIGHT RIDE

BY PAMELA DELL

TRADITION BOOKS™
EXCELSIOR, MINNESOTA

TABLE OF CONTENTS

An eerie howl rose up into the night just as I reached the top of Copp's Hill. It was a sound so hideous and unexpected that I started with fright and stumbled. I looked hastily over my shoulder but could see nothing moving at all. Only the thick, dark shadows of the gravestones. I felt a scream of my own clogging my throat and wanting out. But if those two boys were here already and heard me, that would be the end of it.

I hadn't wished to be prowling about the lonely acres of a burying ground in the dead of night, but I steeled my nerves against turning back. I'd gotten this far now, and I wouldn't be scared off, not by anything. Because I had to know.

I froze as a second howl struck the dark, but then it faded away into a series of long, whining barks. I breathed easier. It was only a dog, and it seemed to be moving away now, rather than closer. No other sounds came. No footfalls, no whispery voices. Neither of them was here yet—I was sure of it.

I wove carefully through the marble slabs, trying not to touch any of them for fear I might wake a body from its cold sleep beneath the earth. At the top of the hill, there was a small clump of trees, their boughs thick with new spring leaves. I took

Copp's Hill, a site overlooking the Charles River, was begun as a cemetery in the 1660s. But more than a hundred years later, the British used Copp's Hill as a place to position the cannon they fired during the Battle of Bunker Hill.

Here Lyes ỹ Body of
Mary Moore Daughᵉʳ
of Capᵗ Richard &
Mʳˢ Mary Moore of
Oxford who Decᵈ
May ỹ 27ᵗʰ 1730.
Aged 19 Years

It was frightening to be up in the Copp's Hill burying ground
at night, but I had to know what the boys were up to.

cover there, feeling I would not be easily detected while watching for the boys' arrival.

The moon was rising above the Charles River now. It loomed like a lopsided round of butter over all of Boston, but its light did not comfort me. It fell in strands through the trees and threw strange shadows across the gravestones. It shone down on the water, making the British warship below, the *Samoset*, look like a dancing demon in the night. I imagined its twenty-six guns eagerly at the

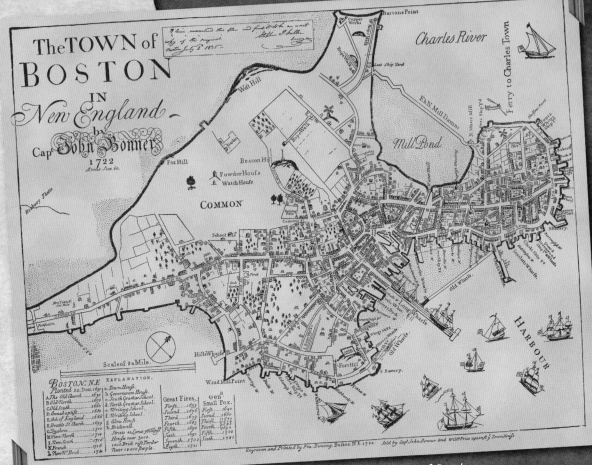

The Charles River was to the north of Boston, and Charlestown was across the river.

King George III of Britain tried to control the American colonies, but we patriots wanted our freedom.

ready to destroy all hopes of liberty for us.

I shivered in the cool April air, trying to ward off the ghostly presence of the dead all around me. I was here, I reminded myself, to help our cause. And that cause was first to keep the living—our living, the colonists, the patriots—from ending up as dead themselves, perhaps run through by a redcoat's **bayonet.** And even greater a cause, to claim our liberty from King George III and all of Britain.

Father and Mother had made us all to understand that every patriot was important to the fight for freedom, right down to the sons and daughters, including my sisters and brothers and me. They had taught us that we were all—every patriot in all the thirteen

9

American colonies—fighting to keep control over our own destiny. And spying for such a cause could bring a person even to hide among the dead if she had to.

As I huddled in the dark, I kept reminding myself of these facts. It was for this I was defying my parents. I had snuck from my bed and up this dreary hill for good reason. Father himself had been one of the men who had thrown hundreds of crates of the East India Company's tea into the waters of Boston Harbor on another dark night, all in the name of liberty. That had occurred on December 16, 1773, exactly sixteen months earlier to the day, and every day now the fight grew more determined.

British soldiers were called redcoats because of the bright red jackets that were part of their uniforms.

"We'll destroy every bit of that tea rather than pay taxes on it to the British!" Father had proclaimed to us before setting out for Griffin's Wharf that night. He was blackening his face with coal dust and sticking feathers in his hair. When we had laughed at his disguise, he chanted to us with a mischievous scowl, "Rally, Mohawks! Bring your axes! Tell King George we'll pay no taxes on his foreign tea!" And then he had slipped into the dark street and was off to the Boston Tea Party.

That event had been a brave deed in the struggle for freedom. So was lurking in the midnight land of death if need be, was it not? So even if my parents were to discover my

Dressed as Indians, a group of colonists made the British furious by dumping tea into Boston Harbor.

Before the Revolutionary War, America was just a group of thirteen colonies. After the war, those colonies became a new nation.

absence, how could they punish me?

I strengthened my spirits with these thoughts as I waited, barely daring to let a single breath escape my lips. Why did those boys not hurry and appear? Had I heard wrong? Were they not after all planning to meet here? In between these questions, though, the worrisome voices of my parents kept forcing themselves upon my mind.

"Mary Cates!" my mother would cry if I were found out. "No young girl should be wandering alone at this time of night!"

"And to Copp's Hill yet?!" my father

At Griffin's Wharf, people cheered at the sight of the Boston Tea Party taking place.

Years before the Boston Tea Party, the British troops angered the patriots by firing their guns into a crowd. Many were wounded and five unarmed patriots died. The incident was called the Boston Massacre by rebel leaders.

Paul Revere was always kind to me, and he was a fine and respected silversmith.

would boom, barely believing it. "Girl, go to your room and I shall deal with you later!"

I turned my attention to recalling again the incident that had occurred the day before. The incident that was the cause of my being in this burying ground in the first place. It had happened at Master Revere's Silver Shop. Paul Revere was known as the best silversmith in all of Boston, and through the good fortune of his friendship with Father, my wish to be employed as a silver polisher in his shop had been granted. It was a job I was proud of, for not many girls were taken in for such a position, especially at twelve years. I worked hard and happily in between my studying hours.

The day before I had been especially

enjoying my work for, instead of hand polishing, I had been given the more advanced task of using the **plenishing hammer** to finish a set of beautiful sugar spoons. My job was to tap gently with the hammer to smooth out the rough forging marks left on the spoons in the process of shaping them.

Finding I needed a smaller hammer to work on the delicate spoons, I went in search of one in a small side room of the shop. I quickly found the tool and was about to leave the room when I heard someone speaking in a low voice just on the other side of the wall. I recognized it to be Mick, one of Master Revere's many **apprentices.** Someone else replied and, in catching a few bits of their

Paul Revere & Son,

At their BELL and CANNON Foundery, at the North Part of BOSTON,

CAST BELLS, of all fizes; every kind of Brafs ORDNANCE, and every kind of Compofition Work, for SHIPS, &c. at the fhorteft notice: Manufacture COPPER into SHEETS, BOLTS. SPIKES, NAILS, RIVETS, DOVETAILS, &c. from Malleable Copper.

They always keep, by them, every kind of Copper faftening for Ships. They have now on hand, a number of Church and Ship Bells, of different fizes; a large quantity of Sheathing Copper, from 16 up to 30 ounce: Bolts, Spikes, Nails, &c of all fizes, which they warrant equal to Englifh manufacture.

Cafh and the higheft price given for old Copper and Brafs.   march 20

Master Revere worked in brass and copper in addition to silver.

Revere possibly had as many as eleven brothers and sisters.

14

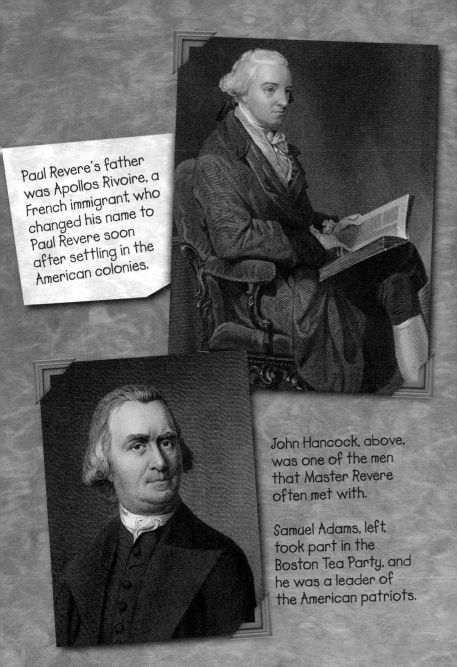

Paul Revere's father was Apollos Rivoire, a French immigrant, who changed his name to Paul Revere soon after settling in the American colonies.

John Hancock, above, was one of the men that Master Revere often met with.

Samuel Adams, left, took part in the Boston Tea Party, and he was a leader of the American patriots.

sentences, I stopped and began to listen more carefully. In a moment I was shamefully **eavesdropping.**

"—have to find out exactly where the rebel leaders are hiding. Especially John Hancock and Sam Adams," said the voice I did not recognize. "You can help us by watching every move Paul Revere makes, as he might lead us to them. The general will pay you a **shilling** for every useful piece of information. Agreed?"

I heard Mick chuckle in a husky, prideful way. "Done," he said.

I stood on the other side of the wall, nearly in shock. Mick, a **Tory?** A Loyalist? I could barely believe it was true. He was forever going on about the patriots and how it was time the colonists took what was rightfully theirs. How we had endured enough hardships at the hands of the British. Was I misunderstanding what I was hearing now, or was Mick's loud talk just a mockery of the patriot struggle? My fingers trembled and for a moment I feared I would drop the hammer and be found out.

"They call themselves the Sons of Liberty," the other said in a scornful voice. "But soon we shall be calling them the Sons of Captivity!" My stomach turned to hear them laughing together quietly.

"Meet me at Copp's Hill tomorrow evening, an hour after moonrise," Mick said

American patriots Samuel Adams and John Hancock both later signed the Declaration of Independence, a document that proclaimed America's freedom from the British.

softly. "I shall have something to tell you by then."

Their footsteps faded. I waited several minutes, then slipped out of the little room and came around into the main workshop. Mick was again seated at his bench, his back to me. Standing before him was a tall blond boy who, like Mick, appeared to be about sixteen years old. His eyes met mine as I sat to resume my work.

"Well, Mr. Cunningham is awaiting his **tankard,**" the blond boy said loudly, grabbing a large lidded mug from where it stood on Mick's bench. "Thank you for the quick repair, sir. You can put it on my master's bill."

Paul Revere learned to be a silversmith by apprenticing with his father.

Mick pretended to be repairing a tankard like this one after I overheard him talking to the tall blond boy.

Mick nodded, saying nothing, and, as if he were a complete stranger, the boy was gone without another word.

I focused my eyes on the spoon in my hand, but I was suddenly deadly determined to know what Mick was up to. It was then that I vowed to face Copp's Hill in the dark—to become a spy myself.

———◆———

But once I'd actually hidden myself in that shadowy burying ground, every minute of waiting made me want more and more to be gone from that place. I'd had more than enough of the haunted voices of wind swirling about me. Nearly more than I could take of the great anxious waves curling through my stomach for fear of what might occur should Mick and the other boy discover me.

And then it came. A strange, low whistle—one long note. In reply, another whistle sounded, this time two short notes. There came the sound of slow and determined feet, and a few yards off I saw a slim, shadowy form that I recognized to be Mick. Another dark shadow emerged from the trees a few feet below him. They began to speak in hushed voices, but the wind was not in my favor. I would have to move closer to hear their words.

Biting my lips together and stepping as carefully as I could to make no sound, I crept dangerously near. The blond boy was speaking.

John Hancock was president of the Continental Congress from 1775 to 1777.

18

"—a surprise attack," he was saying. "General Gage intends to find out just how much **ammunition** they are storing up in Concord and thereabouts. What have you learned?"

"I have been watching Revere as best I can to discover his actions," Mick replied. "Just this morning, though it be Sunday, I went to the shop on the excuse that I had left my cap there. I was nearby when Revere brought his horse from the stable and told his wife he was out for a ride up that way. Lexington, he said. But to what purpose I know not yet."

The Tories reported to this man, General Thomas Gage.

"Why did you not follow?" the boy hissed. "He might have led you straight to Hancock!"

Mick's voice took on a defensive tone. "Today is the Lord's day, Henry!" he said. "I would have followed, but my father had commanded me to return immediately home after fetching my cap. I was made to spend the entire morning reading Bible chapters to my sisters. There was no way out of it."

Henry laughed scornfully. "If you obey at every turn, there is not much use for you to us," he said.

"Mark tomorrow's date," replied Mick, sounding more confident than I believed he truly was, "Monday, April 17, 1775. By the end of tomorrow, I will prove to General Gage my worth. I will send word to you detailing exactly what Paul Revere is up to. I swear I will uncover information that will help to defeat the Yankees once and for all."

"He is one of only two known rebel leaders left in Boston town," Henry whispered harshly. "So you best be correct in your details. As I have already told you, the troops march out on Tuesday night. At all costs, those two **trea-sonous** donkeys must not be alerted of this."

After the Boston Tea Party, King George was furious. He wanted someone to control the American colonists, so he named General Thomas Gage, the commander in chief of British forces in the colonies, to be the new governor of Massachusetts. General Gage was sent to Boston with troops.

"I shall **thwart** every move," Mick vowed. "I shall send news to you at Mr. Cunningham's through Revere's messenger boy."

Mick paused as the old clock in Christ Church struck ten, then added, "When you receive my note, Henry, mind that you read between my lines," he said.

In my hiding place, I suddenly felt something slither across my foot. Startled, I stepped back in the dark. A twig snapped. The boys immediately went still, and from the shadows I saw their heads turn in my direction. I dared not breathe.

The Green Dragon Tavern was a popular meeting place for American patriots.

"It was nothing," Mick said finally. "Except perhaps a skeleton out for a stroll."

"No time to be joking," Henry replied. "Are you sure you weren't followed?"

"Absolutely. But I shall be away now, or my absence will be noticed."

"If you have further news after tomorrow evening, meet me Tuesday noon at the Green Dragon Tavern. We suspect that is where the rebels plot and plan, and we are now all over that place in watch. I shall be taking dinner there."

"Right," said Mick, and then they were gone.

———————

Stealing home, I was relieved to find my entire family fast asleep. No one heard me slip into bed. In the dark before sleep, I weighed whether I should tell my parents what I had heard. But if I told them, I knew they would immediately take things out of my hands. I would no longer be able to be a patriot spy. I fell into sleep vowing I would tell no one until I learned exactly what Mick had found out.

As I worked quietly in the shop the next day, I stayed out of Mick's way, but kept a close eye on his movements among the other apprentices. I kept recalling a trou-blesome thing he had said to Henry. What exactly had he meant by the words, *"read between my lines"*? I concentrated on trying to untangle the meaning of those mysterious words.

Read between my lines. Was he saying that he would ask the messenger to relay to Henry a verbal message that held a secret meaning? Would he write words that would really be a code already known between the two of them?

Thinking hard on this problem, I rubbed furiously at the cream pot I was hand polishing. It had been in the fire so many times during its shaping that it was deeply **tarnished.** But as I polished, it began

Soldiers in the American colonies were called Yankees by the British troops.

to shine with fine, silver light. And then, in the same way the sterling glow appeared out of the tarnished surface of the pot, the secret of Mick's words revealed themselves to me. I knew exactly what he had meant, I was certain.

When, late in the afternoon, Mick finally called for Joe Frost, the messenger, I was ready. Mick handed Joe a small cloth bag and gave him instructions, then Joe left by the front door. I quickly tidied up my work space and made an excuse to the silversmith who was in charge in Master Revere's absence, saying I had an errand to run for my mother. I slipped out the back and wound through the alley to catch up with Joe safely away from the shop.

Revere's work as a silversmith was well respected during his lifetime and for many years to come.

Wisely, I had tied a **pocket** around my waist that morning, though usually I did not wear pockets to the shop. Inside it I had placed six **pence,** ready to make my plan a success. There was something else inside it as well now, something I had borrowed from the shop and which would be equally important if my hunch was right.

Joe was not surprised when I greeted him and, being a little lazy, was much pleased when I offered to do his errand for him.

"I am going just by the Cunninghams' myself, so I should be glad to drop off the package for you," I told him. "But it won't do for you to go back to work too soon, for they would be all full of questions."

In addition to being a silversmith, Paul Revere also served as a dentist in Boston.

It was through these streets that I managed to catch up with Joe Frost and intercept Mick's message.

Joe nodded agreement.

"So you can do something for me, too," I said as I drew four pennies from my pocket. "Go to the sweet shop and get me some peppermints, all right?"

"Peppermints?" Joe's eyes lit up, and he looked down at the coins.

"Yes," I said, "two pence worth for me and two pence for yourself. But you must promise never to tell anyone that I am doing your work for you, right?"

"Right-o, Mary!" said Joe, with a wide smile. "Mum forever!"

The minute he was gone, I ducked down a narrow alley and settled on the stoop in a deserted doorway. I drew out the sugar **urn** and checked inside the bag but found no note there. The urn itself was one of Mr. Revere's finest designs, with a delicate, tight-fitting lid. I lifted the lid, but the urn was empty, too. Inside the lid, however, I found what I had been looking for. Mick had cleverly added something extra to his handiwork. It was a thin lip of silver encircling the inner lid. Pushed into the narrow curved space between that silver lip and the lid itself was a strip of **parchment.**

Carefully I pulled the page from its hiding place. I unfolded and smoothed the thin parchment on my lap and was not surprised to see a scrawled note in Mick's hand. It read, "Herewith the sugar urn ordered by Mr. F. Cunningham. Cream pot shall be delivered in three days. Cordially,

Revere Silver Shop."

I could hardly see any code in those words. Except for the mention of "three days," it was altogether unsuspicious, in fact. Even three days meant little if the British were truly planning to strike the following night.

I looked up and down the lane to be sure no one was about. Then turning my back to the street and bending into the corner of the doorway, I proceeded with my plan. From my pocket I withdrew the two things I'd gathered at the shop: a stump of candle and a flint for lighting it. When the candle was burning in the windless corner, I held Mick's note above the flame with the greatest care. I held it just high enough so that it would be warmed but not burned. In seconds the page began to grow darker, becoming a soft brown color in the heat. As it darkened, I saw what I was looking for. Ghostly letters began to appear beneath the already-existing lines of Mick's note. I was right! The page held a second, more **sinister** message. Between the visible lines, Mick had written a secret note to Henry using invisible ink!

Father, being a **chemist,** had shown us only a few months earlier, how to make such ink. It was, he said, a fine way for sending important messages without the enemy discovering their true contents. As we watched, he had mixed something he called **ferrous sulphate** with water. Then using a quill pen, just as normal, he wrote upon parchment. We could see not a word there,

By heating the parchment, I discovered
the real message Mick had written.

Quill pens were made
from the feathers of
birds, such as geese
or swans.

but when he held the page above a glowing candle, his script miraculously appeared. Now I had succeeded in doing the same there in the doorway.

Mick's secret message made my heart pound. I could barely comprehend the evil meaning in his words. It read, "Revere knows. Plans to alert minutemen and every village north of Boston when Gage's troops march. I shall be his shadow tomorrow evening, and he shall meet his Maker before he is able to warn a single soul." There was no signature to this note—only a skull and crossbones.

My mind whirled as I wondered how he could have gotten this knowledge. He clearly had spies of his own. I thought of Dr. Church, whose family lived next door to

A minuteman, one of the colonial soldiers ready for battle

British troops had landed at Boston with a fleet of ships.

Mick's family. Dr. Church was a member of the Committee of Safety, formed by the patriots to organize against the redcoats. But I had recently overheard Father telling Mother that none of the Sons of Liberty trusted him anymore. Could Mick be somehow getting information from Dr. Church? I had no time to think it through.

I refolded the note and slid it into my pocket. I put the pot into its bag and gave a boy on the street my last two pennies to deliver the package to its owner, without Mick's note. As I hurried away, my stomach was curling in knots again. I longed to be at home and under the covers in my safe little bed, to stay there until we were rid forever of the British. But at the same time, there was a fire burning in my mind. The next day was April 18, the day Henry had said the British would march out. I knew what I had to do, and I would do it.

———

My first hope had been to alert Master Revere myself of what I had discovered. But he did not appear in the shop the next day until near evening. Fearful of arousing

In 1774 and 1775, Paul Revere served as an express rider, carrying messages, documents, and news from Boston to New York and Philadelphia.

Mick's suspicions in any way, I waited until his eyes were busy elsewhere. The moment he put his **crucible** into the fire to melt a bar of silver, I got up my nerve and hurried to Master Revere. He smiled kindly, but before I could utter a word of warning, he said he had much on his mind and whatever I needed would have to wait. Then he hurried out. Shortly Mick left as well. I had to follow.

———

It would have been comical to me had it not been so terrifying. It was well after dark when I slipped from the shop to follow Mick. That morning I had told Mother I'd been invited to supper by Master Revere's daughter Sarah,

Revere had sixteen children—eight with his first wife, Sarah Orne, and eight with his second wife, Rachel Walker.

Sarah, Master Revere's daughter, had invited me to her home for dinner on other occasions. Although it shamed me, my mother would not suspect that I had other plans that evening.

who was close to my age, so they wouldn't be expecting me at home. It had shamed me to lie, but I felt my actions would later justify this small untruth. So, feeling part of a desperate chase, I followed Mick at a distance as he followed Master Revere through the maze of North Boston alleyways.

All about me candles were being lit in windows. But there was something else happening. Something that filled me with dread, for down all the streets now, no end of troops began to appear. Hoards of red-coated soldiers, stiff but determined, marching in columns toward Boston Common. Henry's information had been correct. They were on their way.

I picked up my speed, deciding to risk

getting closer to Mick. But all at once, a line of soldiers abruptly cut a corner in front of me and I shrank back against a stone wall. By the time they had all marched past, Mick had completely disappeared.

"No!" I screamed aloud, but the noise of booted steps muffled my cry. I rushed on, turning this way and that down lane after lane, but neither Mick nor Master Revere were to be seen. I had lost them. I had failed.

I could barely breathe from both my frantic running and my disappointment. My side ached, and my heart felt numb. I had reached the banks of the Charles River, and I sat to rest on a low stone wall. Again, just as two nights earlier at Copp's Hill, I heard the clock of Christ Church strike ten. Looking up, I could see the church **belfry** shadowed in darkness.

In the deep stillness of the evening, I heard the sound of footsteps suddenly drawing near the waterfront. Not wanting to be seen, I hurried across the cobblestones and hid myself in a space carved into the building wall facing the water. From there I could see a figure hurrying toward me in the dark. It was Master Revere!

Just as I was about to step out and stop him, I saw, farther back, Mick's thin form moving with caution along the wall after him. I felt the panic rise, but I had to think—and think fast.

British troops and American soldiers fought at Lexington and Concord on April 19, 1775. These were the first battles of the Revolutionary War.

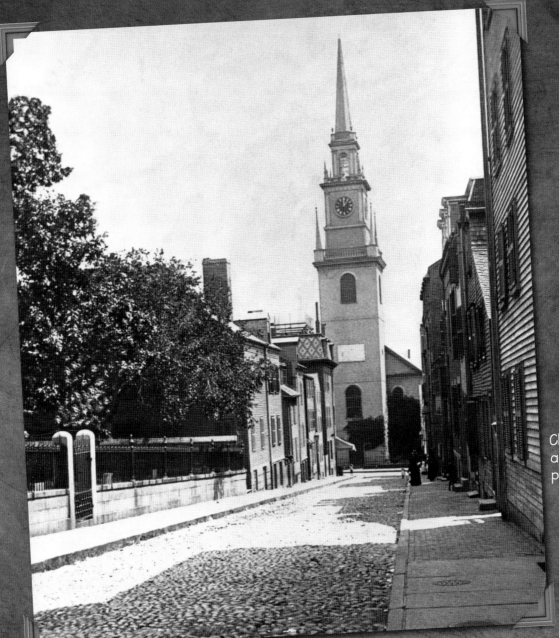

Christ Church was a beacon to the people of Boston.

There was an old rotting stick of wood lying on the cobblestones. I bent and grabbed it. With wildly beating heart, I watched as Master Revere passed me unnoticed and then as Mick approached. Just as Mick came upon where I stood, I crouched again and, holding the stick in two hands, swung it as hard as I could at his ankles.

The wood was soft from being water-logged, and it splintered against his legs as it struck him. He cried out, more from surprise, I was sure, than from pain. But not expecting the blow, he lost his balance and the next second splattered to the ground, cursing. I ran.

Master Revere was just getting into a rowboat with two men as I neared him. He looked back at the sound of my running feet, and a puzzled expression came upon his face as he recognized me. Without waiting, I blurted to him everything I knew, and I pointed back at Mick.

Mick had picked himself up, and when he saw me directing Master Revere's gaze to him, he fled away into the dark. As the sound of his footsteps faded, the absolute stillness of the night descended again. Out in the river the *Samoset* floated, an evil presence standing guard.

"You are a true patriot, Mary, my girl," Master Revere said, his voice low, as if fearing detection. "I will reward you for this—and see to Mick—when I return. But until then, rest assured the enemy will not

When I saw the two lanterns lit, I knew that freedom was soon to come.

take us by surprise. Now look there."

He pointed above to the dark church belfry.

"When you see the signal we have put out, you will know we are way ahead of them, no matter which route they choose to come after us. 'Tis one if by land, two if by sea." Master Revere stepped into the little boat, and one of his companions splashed an oar in and out of the water, readying to make off. The sound was startlingly loud in the quiet night. I feared that even this small sound would be detected by the *Samoset* as Master Revere's boat ferried across to Charlestown.

"Wait!" I called in an urgent whisper. "Take my shawls to muffle the sound of the oars!" Master Revere, still standing in the boat, smiled broadly as I tossed him my cloaks. He caught them with perfect ease.

"Your father will be proud," he said softly. "Now go and be safe."

But I could not leave immediately. I watched the men in their small boat as they moved soundlessly through the deep waters. I watched until I could see them no more.

Finally I turned to go. High above me in the bell tower of Christ Church, I noticed now the glow of a single lantern light. Then, as I watched, a second light appeared. On the other side of the river, hundreds of Massachusetts colonists would be roused from their beds this night. The minutemen, so named because they would come to the call in a minute's notice, would rally from all

On April 18, 1775, Master Revere rode from house to house on his way to Lexington, warning of the British troops on their way.

The Battle of Concord occurred the day after Paul Revere made his famous ride.

The Revolutionary War lasted until the British finally surrendered in 1781. An official peace treaty was signed two years later.

directions. All would hear of these glowing lanterns, and afterward they would tell of this night for a long time to come.

It was late, but all worry had finally fled from me. In my heart there rose a fierce, blazing certainty as I hurried toward home. There might be a difficult and dangerous struggle to come, but we, the patriots—the Americans—were going to win out against **tyranny**. We were going to be finally free.

THE HISTORY OF PAUL REVERE'S MIDNIGHT RIDE

In 1775, several young people, like Mary Cates, served as spies for Boston patriots in the Massachusetts Colony. It was a dangerous time. Tension had been building between Britain and its thirteen American Colonies. The colonies were far from Britain and had grown used to governing themselves. To increase control over the colonies, Britain had passed a series of strict laws. The colonies protested the new laws, especially those that taxed molasses, tea, and stamps.

In 1775, King George III of Britain declared Massachusetts to be in rebellion and sent in troops to restore order. The Sons of Liberty, led by John Hancock and Samuel Adams, were secretly plotting the rebellion and storing arms in the town of Concord. The king ordered his troops to arrest them and destroy their supplies. On the night of April 18, 1775, about 700 British soldiers marched toward Concord.

Two colonists, William Dawes and Paul Revere, rode on horseback to notify patriots of the approaching troops. First they went to Lexington to warn Adams and Hancock. Then they rode to Concord to alert the colonial militia. They arranged for a signal to be flashed from the steeple of Christ's Church in Boston to alert friends in Charlestown. Two lanterns would mean the British were coming by water, and one would mean they were coming by land. Dr. Samuel Prescott, a third rider, joined Dawes and Revere on the road outside Lexington. He was the only one to make it past the British patrols. Revere was captured by the British but later released. He returned to Lexington to get valuable papers from Hancock's trunk before fleeing to safety.

Because of the courage of patriot Paul Revere and others, the colonies won the war against England and became a new nation. In 1783, after eight years of war, the thirteen colonies became the United States of America.

GLOSSARY

ammunition guns, gunpowder, and other weapons used in attacking or defending a position

apprentices people being taught a craft or a trade by working with an expert

bayonet a large knife that fits on the end of a rifle, used to stab an opponent in close fighting

belfry a tower or a room in a tower where bells are hung

chemist a person who works or specializes in the science of substances; in this context, a pharmacist

crucible a container used for melting metals at very high temperatures

eavesdropping listening to other people talking without their knowing you are listening

ferrous sulphate a greenish gray chemical that can be mixed with water to form an ink that is invisible unless viewed near candlelight

parchment strong, thin material used for writing, much as paper is used today

pence an old-fashioned term meaning the plural of penny

TIMELINE

1734 Paul Revere is born in Boston's North End.

1760 King George III becomes king.

1768 In October, British troops arrive in Boston to reinforce custom laws such as the Stamp Act.

1770 On March 5, five colonists are killed in what becomes known as the Boston Massacre.

1773 The Boston Tea Party takes place on December 16.

1774 On September 5, the First Continental Congress meets for the first time. The Congress meets until October 25.

plenishing hammer a hammer used to smooth out rough marks on silver

pocket a small bag or pouch; almost like a purse

shilling a coin once used in Great Britain and the early American colonies

sinister evil or suggesting evil

tankard a silver or pewter mug with a lid

tarnished stained; having lost shine or color

thwart to oppose and stop someone's plans or actions

Tory a person who was loyal to Britain and King George during the American Revolution

treasonous disloyal, betraying one's country to help the enemy

tyranny the unjust use of power; harsh or cruel government

urn a decorative container used to store and serve items such as sugar

1775 On April 18, Paul Revere makes his famous ride. Fighting begins in Lexington and Concord on April 19. On June 15, the Continental Congress names George Washington commander in chief of the Continental army.

1776 On March 7, the British are forced to evacuate Boston. On July 4, the Declaration of Independence is adopted.

1777 On December 1, the winter at Valley Forge begins for Washington and his troops.

1781 The British surrender at Yorktown on October 19.

1783 A peace treaty between America and Britain is signed in Paris.

1787 The U.S. Constitution is ratified on September 17.

1818 Paul Revere dies on May 10 at the age of eighty-three.

ACTIVITIES

Continuing the Story

(Writing Creatively)

Continue Mary Cates's story. Elaborate on an event from her scrapbook or add your own entries to the beginning or end of her journal. You might write about why Mary was a patriot or what happened to her during the Revolutionary War. You can also write your own short story of historical fiction based on Paul Revere's ride or the events of 1775 that led to the American Revolution.

Celebrating Your Heritage

(Discovering Family History)

Research your own family history. Find out if your family had any relatives living in the American colonies at the time of the Revolutionary War. Were they Patriots or Loyalists? Ask family members to write down what they know about people and events during this time period. Were any of your relatives involved directly or indirectly in the American Revolution? Explain. Make copies of old drawings or keepsakes from this time period.

Documenting History

(Exploring Community History)

Find out how your city or town was affected by the American Revolution. Visit your library, historical society, museum, or local Web site for links to the event. What did the newspapers report? When, where, why, and how did your community take action? Who was involved? What was the result?

Preserving Memories

(Crafting)

Make a scrapbook about family life at the time of the American Revolution. Imagine what life was like for your family or for Mary Cates. Fill the pages with special events, songs, family stories, interviews with relatives, letters, and drawings of family treasures. Add copies of newspaper clippings, photos, postcards, birth certificates, and historical records. Decorate the pages and the cover with family heirlooms, patriotic symbols, maps of Paul Revere's ride to Lexington and Concord, or pictures of the famous landmarks of Colonial Boston.

TO FIND OUT MORE

At the Library

Grote, Joann. *Paul Revere: American Patriot.*
Broomall, Pa.: Chelsea House, 1999.

Kent, Deborah. *Lexington and Concord.*
Danbury, Conn.: Children's Press, 1997.

O'Neill, Laurie. *The Boston Tea Party. Spotlights in American History.*
Brookfield, Conn.: Millbrook Press, 1996.

Sullivan, George. *Paul Revere. In Their Own Words.* New York: Scholastic, 2000.

Wade, Linda R. *Early Battles of the American Revolution.*
Edina, Minn.: Adbo and Daughters, 2001.

On the Internet

The History Place: American Revolution
http://www.historyplace.com/unitedstates/revolution/
For important events and dates in the American Revolution

Paul Revere Biography
http://www.paulreverehouse.org/paul.htm
To learn more about Revere's life

Midnight Rider: A Paul Revere Virtual Museum
http://www.cvesd.k12.ca.us/finney/paulvm/_welcomepv.html
For information about Revere and his famous ride

On the Road

The Concord Museum
200 Lexington Road
Concord, MA 01742
978/369-9763
To visit a museum dedicated to the
history of the American Revolution

The Paul Revere House
19 North Square
Boston, MA 02113
617/523-2338
To tour Paul Revere's historic home in Boston

The Old North Church
193 Salem Street
Boston, MA 02113
617/523-6676
To visit Christ Church, now known as the
Old North Church, the site of the famous signal

ABOUT THE AUTHOR

Pamela Dell has worked as a writer in many different fields, but what she likes best is inventing characters and telling their stories. She has published fiction for both adults and kids, and in the last half of the 1990s helped found Purple Moon, an acclaimed interactive multimedia company that created CD-ROM games for girls. As writer and lead designer on Purple Moon's award-winning "Rockett" game series, Pamela created the character Rockett Movado and twenty-nine others, and wrote the scripts for each of the series' four episodic games. Purple Moon's Web site, which was based on these characters and their fictional world of Whistling Pines, went on to become one of the largest and most active online communities ever to exist on the Net. Pamela lives in Santa Monica, California, where her favorite fun is still writing fiction and creating cool interactive experiences.